Stolen Love

By Joyce Lomax Dukes

2011

Olmstead Publishing

Author: Joyce Lomax Dukes
Transcribed: Alexis Sheppard

Cover picture by Bobby R. King

Olmstead Publishing,
www.olmsteadpublishing.com
apopka@usa.com
Printed in the United States of America

Cover Christine Hammett
Editing by Phyllis Olmstead

ISBN-13   978-1-934194-23-2
ISBN-10   1-934194-23-9

Two17-year-old cousins, Charles and Dru Roxenbury, graduated from high school and were planning to college at the end of the summer to study law. Dru traveled from Promise, California, to Los Angeles to spend a few weeks with Charles.

At the beach, they met two 16-year-old girls that were the best of friends, Ashley Richards and Tiffany McKinley. Charles fell in love with Ashley at first sight and then he lost her. Charles rode back with his cousin to spend time at Dru's home with his aunt and uncle. Nine years later, Charles discovered Ashley again.

Chapter One

Charles and his cousin Dru were very close, they both graduated from high school, and at the end of the summer, they are headed off to different law schools. The seventeen-year-olds' fathers' are brothers. Charles' father, Leland Roxenbury, is an attorney-at-law in Promise, California.

Charles' mother, Charlotte Roxenbury, is a social worker. She was raised on her parent's ranch in Texas. She owns a horse ranch called The Roxenbury Ranch. The Roxenbury Ranch is known for training and breeding the fastest of horses.

Dru drove the Jeep his parents bought him for graduation to visit his cousin Charles. Dru and

Stolen Love

Charles loved riding and caring for the horses. After three weeks on the ranch, Charles rode back to Los Angeles with Dru.

They arrived at Dru's house in the evening. Dru's parents took them out for dinner and a movie, just as they did when the boys were younger.

Dru's father, Andrew Roxenbury, owns a law firm in Los Angeles. Dru's mother, Linda, is a secretary at her husband's law firm.

On Saturday morning, the boys got up, ate breakfast, and went to the beach. Shortly after they arrived at the beach, they noticed two 16-year-old girls.

Ashley and Tiffany were the best of friends. Ashley was shy about meeting boys because of a scar on the side of her face. When Charles and Dru got closer to the girls, Ashley caught Charles' eye and he knew it was love at first sight.

The guys spent hours talking and swimming with the girls. When the girls were ready to go, the boys asked if they could take them to the movies that night. Tiffany and Ashley agreed to go to the movies with them.

The boys drove the girls home from the beach. That evening the boys picked their dates back up to go to the movies.

After the movies, they took the girls back home. Tiffany and Ashley lived on the same street, about eight houses down from each other.

They arrived at Tiffany's house first, the guys mentioned to the girls that they would be going to law schools in different states.

Tiffany said, "Ashley and I are going to law school when we graduate, too. We are applying at the same college."

After talking about it for an hour, Ashley said to Tiffany, "It's getting late, I'm going home. I'll see you in the morning."

Ashley said bye to Dru and Charles. Charles called out, "Ashley, wait. I'll walk you home."

While walking with Ashley, Charles noticed she kept pulling her hair to one side of her face, he asked her, "Why do you keep hiding that scar on your face with your hair? How did you get it?"

She replied, "From a burn when I was four years old."

Charles said, "You are so beautiful to me, I fell in love with you at first sight."

She smiled at him and in a skip and a turn, said, "This is my house. Maybe we will see you on the beach Monday."

He smiled and said, "Yeah, I'd like that."

She went into the house and Charles walked back to Tiffany's house.

Dru and Charles said goodbye to Tiffany and went home.

Sunday morning Charles and Dru went to church with Dru's parents.

At church, Charles saw Ashley sitting with her parents. He waved at her then she waved back.

After the service, Charles and Dru went over to talk to Ashley. Dru saw Tiffany leave with her parents.

Dru's mother called out "Charles and Dru let's go." Charles said to Ashley, "I'll see you tomorrow." And, he left with his family. The boys spent the rest of the day at home.

Monday morning, Andrew and Linda were heading to the office when Andrew told the boys they needed to go to the office about 3 pm that he had something for them to do. The boys agreed to show up at the office, and then Andrew and Linda left for work.

The boys went to the beach at noon and they saw the girls playing in the water. The boys joined the girls and they played in the water with them for a few hours.

Later Tiffany told Dru they would have to go because Ashley's mom was picking them up to go shopping.

He said, "We need to be leaving, too. I'll call you tonight."

Dru and Charles went to the office and his father gave them office work to do that evening, then the family went out for dinner.

At dinner, Charles told them about Ashley, saying, "I know in my heart that I am in love with her. It was love at first sight the day I saw her on the beach!"

His uncle replied, "I have something for the both of you boys to do at the office for the rest of the week that will keep your minds off those girls."

The boys had to work for the week, just as Charles' uncle said.

Friday evening Andrew sent Dru to deliver some papers before he came home. Charles rode with Andrew to the store. Riding down the street with Uncle Andrew, he saw Ashley sitting at the park.

His uncle stopped at the store, Charles said, "Look, Uncle. That's the girl I'm in love with, I'm going over to talk to her."

Andrew said, "I'll see you when I come out of the store."

Charles walked up to Ashley and asked her why she was there.

She said, "Hi, Charles! I like coming to the park to draw and I'm waiting for my dad. He's at the store."

He asked, "What did you draw?" She replied, "Look!" He looked at her book of drawings and said, "These are very beautiful." She told him he could have them if he liked, he said, "Yes, I will always keep them."

Andrew called out to Charles, Ashley said, "I will walk with you. My dad is coming, too." They walked across the street together.

Stolen Love

Charles said, "I will call you tonight." Ashley got in the car with her father. Charles got in the truck with his uncle.

That night after dinner, Charles talked to Ashley on the phone.

When he hung up with her he went to his aunt and said to her, "I know in my heart I truly love Ashley and I feel it every time I see her or talk to her on the phone."

His aunt said to him, "If you truly feel that way then finish college and stay in touch with her, build a life together after school. Just always, let her know how you feel."

Charles said, "But, I don't think she feels this way about me."

Aunt Linda said to Charles, "Time. Always give her time."

That weekend the boys took the girls to the amusement park. They had lots of fun riding on most of the rides and playing the games. The boys spent a lot of time with the girls. Dru and Tiffany were getting very close, making plans for when they finished college.

The next weekend the four of them went horseback riding. Every evening Dru went to Tiffany's house to see her, her parents really liked him. Ashley would talk to Charles on the phone.

She did not really want to get close to him. She only liked him as a friend, but that was enough for Charles.

She went to the movies with him on Thursday, just because Dru was out with Tiffany.

Friday evening Dru talked with Tiffany on the phone. She told him that she was spending the night at Ashley's house since she would be going out of town with Ashley and her parents Saturday morning and that they would be back the next Saturday afternoon.

Dru said, "I will see you in church next Sunday if I don't see you when you get back."

Stolen Love

Dru went into the family room where Charles was, and told him that the girls would be leaving early in the morning with Ashley's parents and that they would be back the following Saturday.

Charles knew he would be leaving that Friday before she came back. Dru said to Charles, "I'll be in my room. I think Mom and Dad have gone to bed."

Charles said, "I'm going to call Ashley, and then I'm going to bed, too."

He did not call Ashley. Instead, he decided to go see her. He wanted to say goodbye and let her know he would be back home when she returned with her family.

He took his uncle's truck and parked it up the street from her house then walked back to her house. Afraid to knock on the door, he saw her through the window putting on her shoes.

Her parents were sitting on the couch. She told them she was going to meet Tiffany. Ashley went out the door; starting up the street, she heard something on the side of the house.

She started to run back inside but Charles grabbed her, pulling her to the side of the house. He wanted to talk to her without her parents seeing him.

It was so dark on the side of the house that Ashley could not see who it was. She started hitting and kicking him. He pulled her to the ground to calm her down, but she kept fighting him.

Charles was saying, "Ashley it's me, I need to talk to you," but she was not listening to him. She was not hearing his voice at all.

She continued kicking and punching him and out of anger . . . he raped her.

Charles could not believe what he had done.

Ashley was crying, he whispered to her, "I'm sorry." but she did not hear him.

She never knew who he was.

Charles heard Tiffany call out, "Ashley is that you?" Charles ran.

Stolen Love

Ashley called out, "Tiffany help me."

Tiffany ran into the house screaming, "Mr. and Mrs. Richards, help!" She ran back outside with the Richards right behind her.

They took Ashley inside. Her father asked her, "What happened?" She told him that someone grabbed her when she went to meet Tiffany and pulled her to the side of the house and onto the ground.

Tiffany asked Ashley if she knew who it was that grabbed her. Ashley whispered, "No, it was too dark." Mrs. Richards took her daughter to the bathroom to clean up.

Tiffany picked up the phone to call the police but Mr. Richards took the phone from her and said, "No, Tiff." Tiffany went into the room with Mrs. Richards and Ashley. Ashley did not want to go to the hospital and did not want to call the police. Tiffany said, "But you were raped, you need to call the police."

She said to Tiffany, "I can't." and pleaded to parents, "Please, Mommy, Daddy. No."

Tiffany just hugged Ashley and Ashley's mother said, "You have to promise us you will never tell anyone, not even your parents."

Tiffany promised Ashley that she would not tell.

The next morning they went on their trip. Ashley told Tiffany never to tell Charles and Dru what happened.

Charles got up the next morning too afraid to tell his aunt and uncle what he had done. Friday came and Charles was extremely ready to go home.

When Charles got on the train, Dru said, "I will tell Ashley good bye for you."

Chapter Two

Summer was finally over, Charles and Dru went off to different Law Schools.

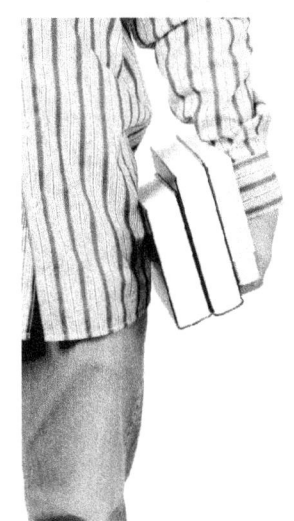

Ashley and Tiffany went back to high school. After two months of school, Ashley became sick and discovered that she was pregnant.

Her parents moved away to the next town. They didn't want anyone to know their daughter was having a baby.

Tiffany kept her promise; they didn't see much of each other.

Ashley found out she was having a girl, and she told her parents she wanted to name the baby Marley.

When the baby was born her parents let the adoption agency take the baby away. Ashley never even got to see her baby girl.

Her parents told her "You are going back to school and to college! Forget you ever had a baby."

Her parents told the agency their daughter got pregnant from a boy that didn't want anything to do with her or the baby. They wanted the baby named Marley Ann.

The Agency knew nothing about the rape.

Ashley finished school; the next year she went off to college to study law, which is where she saw Tiffany again.

She told Tiffany she lost the baby, it hurt her to tell her best friend a lie, but that is what she wanted Tiffany to believe.

Ashley met someone the next summer. He was in medical school, she stayed in touch with him for years.

He was in medical school a lot longer than she was in law school because he was studying to be a plastic surgeon.

The girls graduated from law school and Tiffany went back home and began working in Dru's father's law firm.

Ashley went to Arizona where she married the doctor.

One year later Dru and Tiffany got married, at the wedding Charles asked Dru, "Do you ever see Ashley?"

Dru told him she left here last year and there was talk that she had a baby.

Dru went on to say, "The child was a girl, she put her up for adoption around two years ago." Charles started thinking; he knew the baby had to be his.

Since his father was a lawyer, he would know what to do. Charles went to his parents and told them what he had done.

Charles found out Ashley never reported a rape. She did have a baby girl named Marley and the child was placed in a foster home.

Charles told his parents, "This is no longer my secret. She's my daughter. I can't leave her behind, Mom, I won't." He promised to love and take care of her.

He said, "I loved Ashley then, and I still do, and I will tell my daughter all about her mother." Charles said, "Mom, Dad, please help me get her!"

His parents went with him to the adoption agency, the Roxenbury's told the agency their son didn't know about the baby. So, a DNA test was conducted.

A few days later, the Roxenbury's got a call saying the DNA results were back and to be at the adoption agency in the morning.

Before they left the next day, Charles told his parents that if the test said she was not his baby that he wanted to adopt her anyway because she was

Ashley's child. "I love Ashley. I can love anything belonging to her. I will give the baby the same love as if she were mine own."

His father said, "Let's go see what happens. It would be nice to have a little girl around here." and he winked at his son.

His mother said, "A little girl for me, very nice."

A few hours later they arrived at the agency, a social worker asked them to come into her office. She told them, "The DNA test proved Charles is the father. We got Marley from the foster family and she's here."

The social worker gave Charles the birth certificate to sign. Charles signed his name, and then she said, "Sign here to give Marley Ann a last name." Charles signed Roxenbury and he started trembling.

The social worker said, "She's right through those doors, go get your daughter."

Charles stood up, and then he sat back down. He broke down and started to cry, his mother comforted him. Mr. Roxenbury said to the social worker, "Let's go get her."

He told his wife, "I'll take Marley for a walk. We will be by the car."

Charles cried telling his mother, "It's my fault she didn't want her baby." And, "It's because of what I did to her, Mom. Marley is her daughter, why she didn't want her is entirely my fault."

His mother held him, saying, "Maybe her parents didn't think she was ready for a baby. Don't say she didn't want her, she carried her for nine months. She loved what was growing inside of her. It's not her fault, either. Love her child for her. Teach your baby to love her mother."

After she calmed her son down, they walked outside.

Marley was walking hand in hand with her grandpa, he lifted her in the air spinning her around, and then he ran around in circles with Marley chasing him.

When grandpa saw his wife and son coming, he told Marley, "That's your daddy, let's run to him."

When grandpa said, "Ready, set, go!" Marley took off running saying, "Daddy."

Charles reached down and grabbed her, holding tight to his little girl, telling his mother, "She's mine. She's Ashley's baby.

Marley repeated him saying, "Ashley baby." He continued, telling his mother, "She's beautiful, my beautiful baby."

Charles held his daughter all the way home.

The family stopped in town to go shopping for their little girl. They bought bedroom furniture and everything they needed to fix her room at the ranch.

Grandma took Marley shopping for clothes, shoes, and everything she would need.

Grandpa and Charles said, "We will catch you later. We need to shop for her, too."

A few hours later, she ran into the men coming out of a toy store. While taking everything to the car she asked them, "Did you two buy every doll in the store?" Her husband grinned and said, "Yes we did." They had lunch and headed home.

After Marley's furniture was delivered, they spent the rest of the day putting her room together.

Charles had to be back in school in two days, so he spent the next two days with his daughter. Each night he made a bed on her bedroom floor, he knew when he went back to school Marley will be safe and with people who loved her.

Stolen Love

The morning he left to go back to school, he held his little girl saying, "Daddy loves you, I'll see you soon.

Charles called home every night just to hear her voice and so he could say, "I love my beautiful baby girl."

Marley spent her days with grandma watching her along with the horses. When grandpa came home in the evening, he walked the ranch with Marley riding along side him on one of the colts.

Charles finished that year of law school and came home to his daughter. He continued to live on the ranch with his parents and Marley.

At the age of six, Marley's grandma taught her how to ride a horse. She loved her Saturday morning rides with her father and grandparents.

One year later, Marley, and her father moved into an apartment.

Marley was happy to be with her daddy.

She asked him about her mother, and he told her she would see her mom, he promised. He told Marley just to give her time she would come to her.

Charles made up a bedtime story for Marley, about the summer he met her mother when they were at the beach, went to the movies, and to the park.

Marley went to sleep at night listening to the story of her mom. It was her favorite bedtime story.

Stolen Love

Chapter Three

Two years later, Charles' parents were in a car accident, his father died instantly and his mother was taken to the hospital.

Charles picked Marley up from school and they went to the hospital.

His mother told him to find Marley's mother, murmuring, "She needs to know her mother."

Marley lay in bed with her grandma crying, saying, "Granddaddy gone" and telling her grandma she was scared.

Grandma died later that evening.

A few weeks after the funerals, Charles and Marley moved back to the ranch. Uncle Andrew, Aunt Linda, cousin Dru, and Tiffany drove to the ranch to visit the little family.

They asked Charles about Marley's mom. He said a girl I knew from Promise had her and gave her to my mother and left town, she never came back.

Charles then asked Tiffany about Ashley, Tiffany looked at Marley very strange.

She said, "She's married to a doctor, they live in Arizona. We don't really talk."

So, Charles saw no reason to find her.

At the same time, Ashley and her husband were getting a divorce. Her husband found out she could not conceive and he wanted children.

After the divorce she went to her parents and told them, "I've lost my husband I could never have children. We went to the doctor and found out that you had me fixed."

She cried, "Why did you do that, my husband and I had trying for a year to have a baby?"

She told her mother, "My husband accused me of knowing. I tried to tell him I didn't know but he didn't believe me!"

"He got so angry with me. Now we are divorced because of you. I don't have my husband anymore."

She stormed off saying, "I'm going to bed."

The next morning she said, "I'm going to see Tiffany and Dru. I plan on making a home there but I am going to travel first."

Her mother asked, "Are you going to find Marley now?"

She turned and looked at her mother and said, "You named her Marley, but you wouldn't let me keep her. You just took her away. Why should I look for her now, it's been nine years?"

Her mother gave her all the information she needed, saying, "If you change your mind. . ."

Ashley left her mother and went to the place where her child was placed up for adoption.

She was afraid to go in so she left and went to a hotel to do some thinking.

The next morning, still not sure about going in, she thought about how old the child was, and wondered if the child hated her, and of what she could possibly say to the child.

Ashley finally went into the adoption agency and gave them all the information she had on her daughter.

The clerk came back and said, "The child had been adopted." Then she said, "No, the courts gave the father custody."

Ashley started having flashbacks to the rape, she said, "What father? What was his name?"

The clerk said, "Charles Roxenbury, a DNA test proved that he was the father of Marley."

Stolen Love

Ashley got very angry and went back to her hometown to see Dru and Tiffany. She asked Dru if Charles told him about his daughter.

Dru told her Charles was looking for her about a year ago. "We told him you were married." Dru told Ashley that Charles had lost both of his parents in a car accident, and he and Marley moved back to the ranch.

Ashley shreiked, "Marley!"

Dru said, "Yes. The child's mother gave his parents custody and left town."

Dru started telling Ashley about Charles and Marley, she was getting sick of listening to him talk about how great Charles was with his daughter. She said, "I would like to visit him, how can I find him?"

Dru told Ashley where she could find Charles. The next day she left for Promise. As she was driving and thinking about how nice he acted, how they played on the beach, and all the fun they had that summer. She remembered when he told her he loved her drawings, how he would always keep them.

Then she started thinking about how he attacked her, she hated him for what he did to her.

Now he had stolen her baby!

When she arrived in Promise, she stopped for gas at the gas station.

When she was walking out of the gas station a man snatched her purse and ran with it. She no longer had her ID, money, or phone. He had taken it all.

Ashley got back into her car and drove off looking for The Roxenbury Ranch.

When she saw the police station, she decided to report her purse stolen. As she neared, she asked a man outside of the station, "Do you know where The Roxenbury Ranch is?"

The man answered, "Yes, that's Charles Roxenbury and his daughter over at the feed store."

The man drove away leaving Ashley standing there at the edge of the road.

Ashley called out with anger, "Charles!" she starting walking very fast. By the time, Charles turned to see who had called his name, Ashley had walked out in front of a car and was hit. Charles could not tell who called him, he just saw someone hit by a car.

People ran to help, so did Charles and Marley.

Ashley saw Marley and reached for her and then she passed out.

Ashley was taken to the hospital and she was in a coma for four days. For four days, Marley thought about the woman.

She asked her daddy if he knew her. He said, "I've never seen her before."

Marley thought, "She reached for me, so maybe my mom sent her."

She asked, "Daddy can we go see the lady in the hospital?"

Charles said, "Sure we can."

Charles and Marley went to the hospital; Charles went to talk to the doctor. Marley stayed in the room with Ashley, she remembered the woman reaching for her.

Marley touched Ashley's hand and felt something strange, and then suddenly Ashley woke up. Marley instantly took to Ashley not knowing why.

After she awoke, they found out she had amnesia, so she stayed in the hospital for a few more days.

When Ashley was to be released from the hospital, Marley asked her father, "Can the lady stay with us until she remembers?"

Her dad replied, "Yes, she can stay in the guesthouse." Charles told his housekeeper,

"Someone will be staying in the guesthouse for a while."

The housekeeper replied, "I'll get it ready."

The next day, Charles and Marley brought Ashley home with them.

When they walked in the guesthouse, Marley saw fresh cut roses in a vase by the door. She took one out and gave it to Ashley and said, "This will be your name until you remember yours." Ashley said, "Rose, I'll take it." smiling at Marley.

For the next two weeks, Marley spent a lot of time with Rose trying to help her remember. Marley thought that Rose had a message for her.

They went horseback riding and walked the long horse trails.

Charles brought Rose's car to the ranch, he ran a check on it and found out it was registered to a doctor in Arizona. The doctor was out of the country, and couldn't return his calls.

Charles did not remember what Tiffany told him about Ashley marrying a doctor in Arizona.

The next morning Marley went off to school, Rose asked Charles if she could go to the office with him. She wanted to look around town to see if she could remember why she was there.

When she walked in the law firm, she started having flashbacks, as if she might be a lawyer.

She walked around the office for a while, and then went outside looking around. She didn't know the town, she saw the courthouse and she remember being in a courtroom.

She went back into the law firm, and went into Charles's office and told him, "Maybe I'm a lawyer."

He told her, "Look over this case and tell me what you think."

She came back to his office later that afternoon, and gave him a few suggestions that he liked. She worked at the office for a few months.

He kept winning the cases that she prepared. Charles began to believe she was indeed a lawyer.

One Friday evening Charles told Rose, "I'm checking into something and it will tell me if you are a lawyer or who you are by Monday. In the meantime, let's go home for the day."

Later Marley went to the guesthouse to invite Rose for dinner.

After dinner, Marley asked Rose, "Do you want to see some pictures that I drew?"

Rose answered, "Do you draw?" Marley replied, "Yes, my daddy says my drawing is good and beautiful like my mother's."

Charles went upstairs and left the women to the picture.

While Rose was looking at Marley's drawing and she started to have flashbacks again. Marley asked her, "What's wrong?"

She said, "I'm just tired." Rose took the drawing back with her to the guesthouse.

When she was ready to go to bed, she looked at the drawing again and started having flashbacks of many drawings on a wall in a room. Her room when she was in high school.

She went to bed trying to force herself to remember, but she couldn't, and finally drifted off to sleep.

Saturday morning, Marley asked Rose to go horseback riding with her and the both of them headed off to the barn.

Charles looked out his bedroom window and saw them riding. From afar, Rose looked like Ashley to him, but Charles just shook it off and got dressed.

He went outside and started to talk with the ranch foreman.

Marley's friends from the ranch next door were out riding, also. They asked her to go riding with them.

Rose said to Marley, "You go on; I'm going back to the stable." Rose rode back toward the stable and she saw Charles and the foreman talking.

She handed the horse to one of the stable workers and said to Charles, "Marley is riding with the kids from next door."

She turned away. Charles glanced at her, and had another flashback of the time he walked Ashley home one evening.

He shook off the feeling, again.

Rose went into the guesthouse and started cleaning up. She saw Marley's drawings and she took them to the main house and up to Marley's room.

She sat on the bed and looked at the drawings again. When she went to put them in a cabinet, she pulled out another book of drawings.

When she opened the portfolio she envisioned Charles' face saying, "I'll always keep them."

Suddenly she remembered the rape!

Joyce Lomax Dukes   39

Everything came rushing back like a flood.

"These are the drawings I gave to Charles." she thought.

She went outside and saw Charles walking back towards the house. She stood there in the yard with the drawings in her hands.

Charles walked up to her and she asked, "Where did you get these drawings."

Charles started to remember Ashley, and love started filling his heart. He told her, "A girl I loved long ago gave them to me."

He took the drawings from her, held them to his heart, and said, "I loved her so much and I still do. I think of her all the time."

"I met her one summer when I visited my cousin. It was love at first sight for me."

"One night I hurt her so bad. I will never forgive myself."

He looked at Rose and said, "Rose I just wanted to talk to her and I went to her house. I saw

Stolen Love

her come outside . . . I pulled her to the side of her house so her parents wouldn't see me."

Ashley started to have flashbacks.

"She kept fighting me . . . I kept trying to tell her it was me, but she wouldn't listen. She kept hitting and kicking at me." He turned away from Rose. "Rose, I got so angry that she was fighting that I hurt her. I loved her, I would never hurt her in my right mind, but I did."

"Rose, I don't think she ever knew it was me. It still hurts so bad . . . knowing I did that to her . . . to Marley's mother."

"I found out almost two years later that she had a baby and the child was put up for adoption, I knew the child had to be mine."

Rose was crying the entire time Charles was talking to her. However, he did not know she was crying because he had his back to her.

"Ashley was so beautiful and shy back, then and there was no one else in her life. Therefore, I knew in my heart that Marley must be my little girl. I had to take a DNA test to prove it. Even if the test came back saying she wasn't mine, I would have taken her anyway because she was a part of someone I loved so deeply."

"I was in college when I told my parents what I did to Ashley and they helped me get her. They brought her home to live with them."

"I finished law school that year and came home to my daughter and parents, my family. Such a beautiful feeling, I never told anyone about this, just my parents and now you."

Charles turned around to see that Rose was crying.

He said, "I'm sorry, I didn't mean to make you cry."

Rose spat out, "I hate you."

Charles shouted, "What?"

She said, "You raped me!"

Charles shouted, "What, uh, uh, I , I, never touched you!"

Rose cried out, "I remember! I am Ashley!"

Charles was in shock--pacing back and forth in the yard. Ashley said, "The amnesia, that's why I didn't remember you, but you been looking at me all this time and you didn't know me. Someone you claim to have loved so deeply!"

He said, "You don't look the same! It's been nine years. Your hair is short. The scar on your face is gone! I didn't see it then but I can see it now."

"Little things you did reminded me of Ashley, I saw my daughter getting close to you, but I couldn't do it because you weren't Ashley, and all this time you were."

"My heart has always been yours. I still love you, that is forever!" Then Charles asked her, "Why did you cut your hair? What happened to the scar you always hid with your long beautiful hair?"

She answered, "I married a plastic surgeon, and he removed the scar so I cut my hair."

"We are divorced now because I can't have children, thanks to my mother."

"She had me fixed so I could never have another child." She continued, "I couldn't tell him that I had a child because I didn't want him to know that I was raped."

Charles said, "Please don't say that . . ."

Ashley said, "It's true, you raped me and I had a baby. My mother just took her away, as if she was nothing!"

"I remember her being born, I woke up, and she was gone." Ashley cried. "I never even got to see her . She didn't let me see her! She was mine and she stole her. And now you have stolen her from me, too!"

"The only thing I ever loved! She grew inside of me and I never even got to see her!"

Stolen Love

Charles said, "I just wanted my child, I wanted a part of you."

Ashley said, "So you stole her."

Charles answered, "When you graduated from college, why didn't you look for her? You ran off to Arizona and married a doctor. Why didn't you think to find her first?" Charles suddenly remembered Tiffany saying that Ashley married a doctor and they lived in Arizona.

"That day you were hit by the car, I heard someone call my name but I didn't know who it was, when I turned I saw you get hit. It was you calling me, wasn't it?"

"The man that hit you said you walked out in front of him, you didn't look. When I brought your car to the ranch, I tried to trace it only to find out that it was registered to a doctor in Arizona. I still didn't think about what Tiffany said."

Ashley said, "It was a birthday present from him, that's why it's in his name."

Charles vowed, "If you came here for Marley, I can't let you take her."

"I knew I lost you when I found out you were married, but my daughter is my life. Please forgive me for what I did to you, that wasn't my intention!"

"I love you. I just wanted to talk to you, but not over the phone. I wanted to see you . . . only to hug you and say goodbye, but you wouldn't listen to me."

"I will not let you take my daughter to fulfill your marriage." He added. "She's my daughter not his."

Ashley replied, "My marriage is over. Marley's my life now, just like she's yours."

They saw Marley riding her horse to the stable. Charles said, "We can sit down together and talk to her. All I ask of you is not to tell her about any rape."

"Please don't hurt my baby that way. Please, Ashley!" he begged.

Ashley started to cry again as Marley started skipping towards the house. Ashley dried her eyes and walked out to meet her.

Charles asked Ashley, "What are you going to do?" Ashley kept walking without answering him.

Marley skipped up to her and said, "Hi Rose!" Ashley answered, "It's not Rose, baby. Let's go inside. Your father and I need to talk to you."

Marley anxiously breathed, "You remember, don't you?"

Her Rose answered, "Come on."

Charles opened the door. Marley looked at the both of them, and Ashley rolled her eyes towards Charles.

Marley asked her father, "What's wrong."

He replied to her, "This is Ashley, Baby, your mother."

She said, "Ashley, you do remember! You did come for me!"

"Daddy said you would."

Ashley sat down on the couch. Marley stood in front of her holding onto her daddy saying, "Daddy told me my mother was very young when I was born and still in school. Your mother wanted you to finish school."

"That's why I lived with Grandma and Grandpa while Daddy finished school. When I asked Daddy about you he said I would see you someday. He promised and now you're here!" she exclaimed.

Ashley was shocked that Charles had spoken so highly of her. She looked up at Charles and saw the two people that loved her most in this world were right in the room.

Marley asked, "Are you moving in the house now?"

Ashley said, "I would like to stay in the guesthouse for a while. If that's okay with you, Charles."

He answered, "Yes, that is fine."

Marley said, "When you were in the hospital me and Daddy went to see you. Daddy went to talk to the doctor, and I stayed in your room with you."

"I remember the day you were hit by that car, you reached out for me. So, I held your hand and it felt funny. You squeezed my hand and then you woke up and stared at me. I came everyday to sit with you." Marley recalled.

"When the doctor said you could go home I asked Daddy if you could stay with us until you remembered who you were, and he said you could!"

"The next day when me, and Daddy came to get you, Daddy went to sign you out. I went into your room and you asked me if I was your daughter. I said, 'No.' But, I was wrong!"

Marley started to cry, asking, "Mama, can I hug you?"

Ashley, crying too, reached for her little girl.

Marley climbed in her mother's lap and hugged her saying, "I feel it again."

Ashley saying, "I feel it, too."

Charles kneeled down in front of them and said, "I love you, Ashley. I love you both." Ashley touched Charles face and said to him, "I need time."

Marley looked at her daddy and said, "Remember, Daddy, you said to give her time."

Ashley smiled at Charles.

Marley hugged her father and said, "You promised me I would be with my mother and she's here. Thanks, Daddy."

Charles looked at Ashley and nodded his head yes, then kissed both of his girls on the forehead and said to them, "Let's have lunch."

Marley asked, "After lunch, can we go visit Grandma and Grandpa's grave?"

"I want to tell them my mama is home!"

So, they ate lunch and went to visit his parents' grave.

Chapter Four

Charles and Ashley were sitting on a bench. Marley was at the graves.

Charles told Ashley about his parents and how much his mother wanted him to look for her. He said they loved Marley so much and she loved following her grandpa around the ranch. They would take long evening walks together.

Ashley smiles and says, "Look at my baby, I told Tiffany my baby died. It hurt me to tell her a lie like that."

Charles said, "Tiffany knows. When they came over after the funeral, everyone thought Marley's mother was from around here and left the baby with my parents and took off."

"That's what my mom said to tell them, everyone but Marley."

"One evening, Tiffany asked me to take a walk with her. She asked me who named Marley."

When I said her mother did, she said, "Ashley did."

"Tiffany knew then that I was the one that attacked you that night. I asked her how she possibly knew."

"She said, 'Marley was Ashley's twin sister. She died in a fire when they were four years old.'"

"She said, 'Marley looks like Ashley and Ashley thought the baby died.'"

"She wanted to know how I got Marley. I told her how I found the baby and adopted her."

"I tried to explain that night but she got angry. She said, she would never tell Dru, because that was a promise she made to you. She said you didn't know it was me."

Charles added, "I didn't know you were a twin."

Ashley said, "I really can't remember her, we were only four. That's how I got the burn on my face."

"I only remember her name and Tiffany only remembers what my parents told us. That's how she knew the name Marley."

Charles said, "She told me that no matter what you wanted to do about Marley, she would stand by you."

"Tiffany warmed up to me later. She stays in touch with Marley."

Ashley said, "When I said I wanted to find you she was trying to tell me something. I guess she was waiting for me to tell her."

Stolen Love

"I was so angry with you when I saw you standing with Marley at the feed store."

Marley came back over to where her parents were and asked her father, "Why didn't you know who my mom was when she was in the hospital?"

Ashley said, "I had a scar removed from my face. It made my face look different because the doctors had to pull back the skin on my face."

"I had long beautiful hair like yours."

Then she told her daughter about her twin sister. "That's how you got your name."

Charles said to Marley, "I haven't seen your mother in a long time, but I see her now. I still love what I see."

"Let's go out tonight, we can go shopping. I would love to take my girls shopping and then to the amusement park."

"We can have dinner in town."

They spent the evening out together when they returned home it was late and Marley was sleepy.

She kissed her parents goodnight, then she went upstairs to get ready for bed.

Charles and Ashley talked for a little while longer. They were both getting tired.

Ashley asked him "Could I go upstairs to check on Marley?"

Charles said, "Sure you can." Charles started locking up downstairs.

After awhile he noticed that Ashley never came back down the stairs. He went upstairs and he found her asleep in the bed with Marley. He kissed them goodnight and went to his own bed.

The next morning was Sunday. They had breakfast and went to church together.

When they got back from church, Charles said to Marley, "Let's get changed and check on the colts, and you can feed the animals."

Marley went to change, Ashley asked, "Can I use your computer?"

"I need to check on my accounts because of my purse being stolen and I need to make some calls."

Charles said, "Go ahead."

He went upstairs to change. Charles and Marley went out to the stables.

Later Charles came back in the house and heard Ashley talking to her ex-husband. He told her he had cancelled her credit cards because someone was trying to use them, but that her bank account was okay.

He said that he had been trying to call her for months. He asked her if she was okay.

She answered him, "Yes." She talked with him for a while longer and then hung up and she put her head down on the desk.

Charles asked, "Is everything ok? Are you alright."

She said, "Yes, I'm fine."

She walked to the couch and said to Charles, "You told me that if the DNA test said Marley wasn't your child, you would have taken her anyways because she was a part of me."

Charles sat down beside her, asking, "What's wrong?"

She said, "When we found out I couldn't have kids I told my husband we could adopt. He said he didn't want someone else's child. That he would never take care of a child that was not his." Ashley continued. "All the love I had for him died at that moment."

Charles asked her, "Why didn't you look for her when you finished college?"

"What if I had, not knowing he felt that way?" Ashley laid her head on his shoulder and said, "I'm glad she was with you."

He hugged Ashley and said, "I'm glad you are with us! I love you, and I want us to be a family."

He added, "I want to marry you. I've always loved you."

"Every time I look at Marley I love you even more. If you need time, then, Baby, take your time, but don't leave here."

"I want you here. You can get a job at the firm, anything to keep you in my life."

"I lost you once. That was my fault."

"I don't want to think about that. Let that be our past." he replied. "Can we start now, as a family?"

Marley came in saying she was hungry and sat down on her mother's lap.

Charles kissed Marley on her cheek and said, "You two relax. I'll make lunch."

Ashley told Marley, "I need to go and change clothes. Come with me."

While Ashley was changing, Marley asked her mother "Where are your parents? I've never met them."

"Grandma said that when you came you would tell me about them."

"Do you think one day they will come visit?"

She told Ashley, "I have two sets of great grandparents. They all live in Texas."

"Grams lives on a ranch, too. They are daddy's mother's mama. My other grams don't live far from them, they are granddaddy's parents."

"They all came when Grandma and Grandpa died. Last summer me and Daddy went to visit them. We usually go with Grandpa and Grandma, but it was just me and Daddy last summer."

"Uncle Andrew and Aunt Linda were there. My cousin, Dru, and his wife came, too. Her name is Tiffany, she was very nice to me. She even took me shopping."

"She and Cousin Dru took me and my other cousins to a rodeo. It was fun."

Ashley said, "I know Tiffany, she was my best friend. I went to see her and your cousin Dru before I came here."

Marley exclaimed, "You know Tiffany!"

Ashley said, "Let's go eat, I'll tell you the story about Tiffany and me and how we met your cousin Dru and your Daddy."

After lunch, they went outside on the swings. She told her daughter how they all met that summer. About all the fun she and Tiffany had with Charles and Dru, and that when the summer was over she and Tiffany went back to school.

"It was our last year of high school and your cousin Dru and your daddy went off to college."

"When I found out that I was pregnant with you, I stayed in school until you were born. Later I went back and finished."

"I went to college. That's where I saw Tiffany again. My parents weren't able to keep you so

Charles' parents took you and he finished law school."

"I finished the next year." That's the story Charles told Ashley he told Marley.

She said to Marley, "I met someone else and I married him, but it didn't work out, so we got a divorce."

Ashley continued, "I am so sorry it took me so long to come see you. I glad you were safe."

Marley said, "'That was then.' My grandma said to me , 'When you do see your mother, no matter how long it takes, she doesn't have to explain herself to anyone, it's not her fault, she did nothing wrong. Just remember that, that was then and this is now, and now is what matters.'"

Marley said to her mom "I'm glad you're here."

Ashley hugged her daughter and said, "I love you, and I wish I had had a chance to meet your grandparents. They sound amazing."

Stolen Love

They started swinging. Charles came out to join them, they swung for a while.

Marley said, "Let's walk around the ranch like me and grandpa used to do."

"Daddy, when I get tired you got to carry me on your back like grandpa did."

Dad agreed and said, "Let's go."

They went for a long walk, came back, and watched television together.

That evening they went out for dinner. The next morning Marley went off to school.

Charles and Ashley went to work.

Ashley called Tiffany and Tiffany asked, "Where have you been, I've been calling you for months? Are you back in Arizona?"

She said, "No I'm in Promise, California, with Charles."

"I had an accident, I was in the hospital for a while, but Charles is letting me stay in his guesthouse."

Tiffany says, "Are you alright now?"

She replied, "Yes, but I need to talk to you about Marley."

Tiffany said, "Yes you do, Charles told us a story about a girl from Promise, but I knew that wasn't true."

"When I first saw Marley, she looked just like you, and the name Marley, I knew you were her mother."

"I knew then that Charles was the one that attacked you that night. You told me that your baby died. Why did you say that?"

Ashley said, "I don't know, I thought she was gone and I would never see her again."

"I'm sorry for lying to you," Ashley said.

Tiffany asked, "When you came here, you knew Charles had her then, didn't you?"

She answered "Yes."

Tiffany asked Ashley, "Why didn't you tell me then?"

"I didn't tell you, Ashley, because I wasn't sure if you knew already."

Ashley answered, "I knew you wanted to tell me something."

Tiffany said, "I wanted to call Charles and tell him you were headed there, but then I thought, 'It has been nearly nine years ago and that's between you and Charles.'"

"So, what happens now?" she asked.

Ashley said, "I can't leave her."

Tiffany asked, "What about Charles?"

Ashley replied, "I don't know. I came here so full of hate that I had an accident and ended up in the hospital."

"They both stood by me and I didn't remember who they were. He took me in and cared for me for months."

"When I remembered, at first Charles was shocked, and then he was glad I was there."

"I thought Marley was going to hate me, but so much love poured out of her."

"I wanted him to pay for what he did to me. But through the heart of that little girl he lifted me up so high."

"Right now I don't know what to feel about him, or how to understand him."

"All I know is I'm not leaving my daughter and she's not leaving her father."

Tiffany said, "He loves you Ashley. When I was talking to him, I wanted him to pay, too. But, I think we both know he did."

"I know you see it in Marley." Tiffany continued, "She's beautiful because that's the way her daddy raised her."

"He knew what he was setting himself up for when he got custody. He still didn't care, he wanted her to be with family, and he wanted his daughter."

"What if she was with strangers that didn't love her? So many children are abused by foster and adoptive families."

"He wanted his daughter safe." Tiffany added.

"So, Ashley, what ever you want to do, I'm with you, but I need you to promise me something now."

Ashley asked, "What?"

Tiffany said, "When you left here to go see Charles, I told Dru you were Marley's mom and you got pregnant by Charles, but you didn't put your baby up for adoption your parents did because of your age."

"Dru doesn't know about the attack, so whatever you and Charles decide. Promise me that you will never tell my husband the truth."

Ashley replied, "I think that's best for the whole family. This family is very close and now I'm a part of it."

"But I will stand by you anytime." Tiff vowed.

Ashley said, "I won't hurt Marley. I love her so much and Charles never talked bad about me to her."

"She always believed him and even his parents talked to her positively about me and they didn't even know me."

Tiffany said to her, "They knew you through Charles. They were beautiful people and Marley was their life."

"They were so proud to be her grandparents. It was so hard for her when they died."

Tiffany told Ashley that she had to go because she was due in court and to call her later. They both hung up their phones.

Charles walked into the area where Ashley was working and said, "Hey, you are on the payroll now."

"These are your first two cases, let me know if you need help."

She looked at Charles and he said, "Get your paper work done."

He winked at her, she watched him walk away. All she saw was a strong man that was loving and caring.

She got her two cases set and ready for court. Two weeks later Ashley won both cases.

That evening Charles went into Ashley's office and told her he would be home later because he had a meeting to attend.

Ashley went home to Marley. They had supper together and talked about Marley's day at school.

Marley asked her mom, "Do you want to see some home videos of me that grandpa recorded when I was younger?"

Her mom answered, "I would love to see them!"

They went upstairs to Marley's room and watched the videos together. Ashley started to cry while watching the videos.

Marley asked her mom, "Do you want me to turn it off because I didn't mean to upset you."

Ashley replied, "No, I'm just glad to have the opportunity to see you when you were younger."

Ashley hugged her baby girl and they continued watching the videos.

After an hour, Marley fell asleep and Ashley finished watching the videos that Marley had sitting on the desk in her room.

After she watched them she began putting them back where they belonged and went downstairs to wait for Charles.

Charles came home from his meeting. Ashley told him that she watched the videos of Marley growing up.

Ashley said to Charles, "I'm glad I had the chance to see her grow up on the videos, because I thought I had missed that time in her life." Ashley told Charles, "I'm staying in Marley's room with her tonight."

They said goodnight to each other. Ashley went into Marley's room, kissed her on the forehead, and went to sleep.

Her feelings for Charles strengthened, but she could not tell him, yet she needed to tell someone.

The next morning she told Charles she was driving her car to work because there was something she wanted to do that evening.

That evening Ashley went to Charles parents' grave.

She sat on the ground by the graves. She started talking to his mother, telling her that she was so confused about Charles.

She said that she loved him for the way he raised Marley. But, she hated him for what he did to her.

"I will try to get past that; being around him feels so good. Seeing him with my baby is so beautiful."

"They love each other and they both love me. I love my little girl, it's like you can't love her without loving him because all he ever taught her was love."

"I'll tell you this, I can never tell my mother that I'm with my daughter and her father. She will never understand this."

"You took my child and raised her to be a sweet and beautiful child."

"My mother could have taken her, too." Ashley started to cry. "She didn't even let me see her!"

"She just took her away. That's not what I wanted." She moaned, "She was my baby, I wanted to keep her."

"She didn't stand by me like you did for Charles. When Charles and I were younger, he told me he loved me."

"I'm staying here because of Marley."

"I want to know him. I see now the kind of man he is, loving and kind, but he hurt me."

"When I found out he had my baby, I was so full of hate. When I came to Promise, I saw Charles and Marley at the feed store. I ran out in front of a car. Because I hated him, I wasn't looking!"

"I wanted to take my daughter and let the law handle him. When I was hit, it was like something telling me, 'that's not the right way.'"

"He took me home with him, not knowing who I was. He could have walked away, but he didn't."

"It was as if I needed to know him. If I approached him that day I would have torn down all the love he taught her."

Joyce Lomax Dukes

"I didn't think about what I was going to do to her. I just wanted to hurt him."

"Now I'm having all these feelings for him. It feels good being with him and Marley every evening. But going to bed alone . . . I think about how he hurt me—but—how much he loves me."

"I can't seem to get past the hurt, but I want to. I need something to help me. I'm so lost please help me tell me what to do."

"I need a mother, my mother."

Charles had left work the same time Ashley did.

He stopped and got some flowers to put on his parents grave.

When he got to the cemetery, he saw Ashley's car. He walked up and saw her at his parent's grave.

He stood back and he heard what she said to his mother.

Stolen Love

When she finished talking, she put her hands over her face and began to cry, telling his mother she was confused, and how she really wanted to see her mother.

Charles walked up to her.

She looked at him and said, "Sorry."

He helped her to get up. Then he held her in his arms, he broke down and started to cry. "I'm sorry for hurting you, all your pain is my fault."

"I'll never hurt you again, I love you."

He held Ashley tight. All his pain came back from that day when he heard Marley was his daughter.

They walked over to the bench. They sat down trying to comfort each other.

He told Ashley, "Seeing you hurt, brought back the hurt I felt when the social worker said, 'Go get your daughter.'"

"Those were beautiful words to me, but the way I got my daughter hurt me so badly."

"I made a mistake when I hurt you, but my daughter will never be a mistake."

"I will never be sorry she was born."

Charles looked at Ashley saying. "I know it's hard for you to forgive me. I was wrong for getting that angry with you, I should have walked away."

He stood up and said, "Ashley you are safe with me now. You know that don't you?"

She stood up; they went to put the flowers on the graves. Charles walked her back to her car, then he followed her home.

When they arrived home, they saw Marley riding on the ranch with the kids from another ranch.

Ashley said, "I want to be alone for a while."

Charles replied, "I don't want to leave you alone."

She replied, "I'm okay, just for a little while."

He told Ashley that he would check on her later. He went into the house.

The housekeeper said, "Dinner is on the stove. Marley did her homework, she's out riding. I'll see you in the morning."

Charles went upstairs to take a shower and change clothes.

He came back downstairs and lay on the couch thinking about Ashley and waiting for Marley to come in from outside. Charles fell asleep.

It was getting dark, Marley's friends rode home.

She came into the house and saw her daddy asleep so she went to get a shower.

When she finished her shower, she came downstairs to wake up her daddy.

"I'm ready to eat, Daddy, Do you want me to get mom?"

He said, "No, Baby, she's tired let her sleep. She'll eat later." So, the two of them had dinner.

After dinner, Marley went to her room.

She was online talking with her Aunt Linda and Uncle Andrew. They told her they will be up next month for her birthday.

She talked with them for a while and got on the phone with a friend from school. Charles cleaned up the dinner dishes and lay back down on the couch.

Charles watched television for a couple of hours and then he went to check on Marley.

She was sleeping in her bed. He covered her and turned off the light in her room. He went downstairs to check on Ashley but he did not see any lights on in the guesthouse.

He walked down the sidewalk in the backyard, sat on the swing in the gazebo, and started swinging.

Ashley was sitting in the dark. She heard something out back. She looked out the sliding glass door and saw Charles.

She went out the door and walked down the sidewalk to him. She sat on the swing with him and put her head on his shoulder.

He just kissed her on the head and kept on swinging.

He said, "I'm sorry, I told you that I would never hurt you again, but I was hurting you all along."

"I just didn't want you to leave not thinking about what you wanted, however you want to do this."

"If you want to see your mother I'll stand with you."

"If you want to leave, we can work something out with Marley."

Ashley replied, "I love it here. I love being with you and Marley."

"I don't want to leave you. I know you love me and I know I don't want to spend another night without you."

"I felt that when you held me at the cemetery today, so safe and so protected. Ashley continued, "As for my mother, the three of us can face her together."

Ashley stood up and they walked into the house together. She spent the night with Charles. The next morning Ashley and Charles came downstairs together.

As Marley got dressed for school, Ashley went out the back door to the guesthouse to get ready for work.

When Ashley got dressed, she and Charles left for work. On the way there, they dropped Marley off at the bus stop.

Charles said to Marley, "When we get home tonight, we are going to plan your birthday and something else we need to plan."

Marley asked, "Our trip to Texas to see Grams?"

Charles answered, "No something else."

She said, "What else?"

He said, "Maybe a wedding."

She said, "Yours!"

He shook his head yes, and she looked at her mother and said, "Really?"

Ashley answered, "Yes."

Marley asked, "Tomorrow is Saturday, can we go out tonight?"

"That's my bus, see ya' later!"

When Ashley and Charles got to work, she emailed Tiffany telling her she and Charles were getting married and to call her later.

When Tiffany came in her office, she saw the email Ashley had sent her. She told Dru and his parents.

Ashley and Charles day ended sitting around making plans for their wedding.

Ashley did not want a big wedding because she would not have her father to give her away. It will only be Charles's family.

Marley asked her father "When is the wedding?"

He told her sometime after your birthday.

Marley said, "If it's going to be just family, why not in Texas on Grams' ranch."

"We can ask them, we go there anyway with Uncle Andrew and Aunt Linda every June." Charles said, "We will make some calls Monday morning."

"I have something special planned for tonight. Let's get ready, it's a surprise, and you'll need an overnight bag."

The surprise was that Charles was taking them on a cruise.

Three weeks went by and the plans were made for the June wedding in Texas.

One month later, the weekend of Marley's birthday, her family was due to be in on Saturday morning. The party would be starting at 3 pm out by the lake.

Cousin Dru and Tiffany arrived first. Then an hour later Uncle Andrew and Aunt Linda arrived for the party.

Marley introduced them to her mom.

Uncle Andrew said, "I remember Ashley. It's been a long time!" and he hugged her.

Aunt Linda said to Ashley, "All I remember about you is…It was love at first sight." pointing at Charles.

Everyone sat around talking about the wedding.

At 1 pm, they setup Marley's party. Everyone except Tiffany and Marley helped. They went outside to swing on the swings. The party started at 3 pm. The children ran about having fun.

Uncle Andrew said to Marley, "You invited a lot of children didn't you."

Smiling at her Uncle Andrew, she said to him, "The more children, the more gifts."

Tiffany and Ashley walked to the gazebo and sat on the swing.

Ashley told Tiffany, "I really want my parents at my wedding because they weren't at my first one. I would love to walk down the aisle with my dad, but how can I explain this to them? What would they do?"

Tiffany answered, "What can they do! Charles did a better job than they did. Don't worry, it will work out."

They walked back to the party in time to see Marley open her gifts.

Uncle said again, jokingly, "That's a lot of gifts."

She looked at her Uncle and smiled; "Marley loves all of her gifts."

The ranch foreman came up and said, "Special delivery for Marley Roxenbury."

It was from Great Grandpa. Her very own saddle. He made it just for her. She looked in the bottom of the box and saw a small box from Grams. When she opened it, there was a necklace with a charm of a girl riding a horse.

Marley loved all her gifts from her party and thanked all of her friends and family.

Mom and Dad brought three go-carts. The children took turns riding around the ranch.

At 6 pm, the party wound up and the family sat around talking. It starting getting late, so Uncle Andrew and Aunt Linda stayed in the guesthouse, and Dru and Tiffany slept upstairs.

Early Sunday morning the family got up and went to church together, after church they went out for dinner.

That evening all their loved ones went back home. Everyone said their goodbyes and let them know that they would be seeing them in two months.

Chapter Five

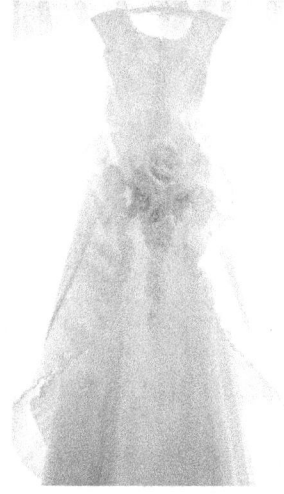

Five days later,
Tiffany went to see
Ashley's parents.

They were very happy to see her. She greeted
them and told them she needed to talk with them.

She told them that Ashley found out Marley
had been adopted; sort of, and that Ashley went
looking for the family that adopted her. Tiffany
continued telling Ashley's parents, "She found them
but there was an accident and she lost her memory."

"The family that had Marley took Ashley in
and when she started to remember, she realized that
Marley was loved and cared for."

"She stayed with the family to be with
Marley." Tiffany said, "Do you remember when we

were in high school, she was going out with Charles Roxenbury?"

Mrs. Richards said, "Yes, he was a sweet boy."

Tiffany said, "You know Charles loved Ashley so much, he always said he was going to marry her. Well, when he found out the baby was put up for adoption, he got the baby and took her home with him because she was a part of Ashley and he waited for Ashley all those years. He loves Marley."

Mr. Richards asked, "So he adopted Marley?"

Tiffany replied, "Sort of."

Mrs. Richards asked Tiffany, "Why do you keep saying…sort of?"

Tiffany answered, "Charles is Marley's father."

Mr. Richards said, "You think we would try to take her. If he adopted her, then he is her father."

Tiffany said, "Mr. Richards, Charles is Marley's biological father."

He said, "Tiff, Charles attacked my daughter . . . he raped my little girl . . . and you're telling me he loved her?"

Tiffany replied, "He still does, and she loves him. They are getting married. We talked about this and it's what she wants."

"When she lost her memory she got to know them both, Marley is happy that her mother is home and she doesn't know about what happened to her mom just that her mother and father are together now."

Mrs. Richards asked, "How old is Marley now?"

Tiffany answered, "She just turned 10, five days ago."

Mr. Richards said, "My baby girl is really happy, she really wants to be with this man?"

Tiffany said, "Yes, she loves him and your

granddaughter but what she would love the most is for her father to walk down the aisle with her."

Mr. Richards exclaimed, "You've got to be kidding!"

"I know it's hard. But, can't you forgive Charles? She did."

"Let her be happy because her first marriage didn't work out. She has a daughter to complete this marriage."

Mrs. Richards looks at her husband and said to him, "Charles took the baby because he loved Ashley. We put the baby up for adoption because we loved Ashley. Which one of us did the right thing? Which one of us hurt her the most?" Mrs. Richards continued.

"The shame that Charles felt is no different from the shame that I am feeling right now. I took her baby away and we both knew that she wanted to keep the baby."

"I haven't seen my baby in almost a year. I thought she was angry with me. I need to see my child."

Mr. Richards said, "Okay." to both his wife and Tiffany."

Tiffany told them that the wedding was going to be held June 19th in Texas on Charles's grandparent's ranch and that it was all Marley's idea.

"You two will be my surprise. I will make all your arrangements and I will get back with you. And one more thing, your trip is on me."

Tiffany talked with the Richards for a few more hours, everyone agreed that the past was the past, and she told them just how she wanted to surprise Ashley and Marley.

When Tiffany left the Richards home, she called Charles and told him about the Richards and the surprise.

Charles called his grandmother and told her about Tiffany's surprise.

Five weeks went by and suddenly it was June 10th.

Uncle Andrew and Aunt Linda were in Texas visiting his parents. They were staying until the wedding.

Dru and Tiffany arrived on the 15th. They went to see Charles, Ashley, and Marley at Charles grandparents house.

Dru said to Charles' grandma, "Tiffany and I will stay in your apartment."

Grams replied, "No, you will stay in the house, my apartment is for my surprise guest."

Dru asked, "Who?"

Grams answered, "If I tell you it won't be a surprise." They all smiled at what Grams said. That night Andrew and Linda came over with his parents,

Charles other grandma. Charles introduced Ashley to them and they loved her right away.

Marley ran to her other grandparents telling them about her birthday, they all had dinner and talked with each other.

Grandma, Charles mom's mother, called Ashley to her room and told her she had something for her.

Grandma said, "My daughter gave this to me years ago to put in the family safe. It was to be given to Marley when she came of age, and if she wanted to find you, Marley was to give it to you without reading it."

"I know what's in it, my daughter and I have known the secret, but before you read it there is something I want you to see."

Grandma showed Ashley the tape of Charles graduating from college, she put it on the part where Charles was giving his valedictorian speech.

She wanted Ashley to hear his speech, it was all about Marley, and when he was walking out with his classmates, Marley ran up to him.

She wanted Ashley to see the look on Charles's face when he picked her up. Grandma stopped the tape and said, "I will leave you to your letter."

Grandma left the room and joined the rest of the family.

About 15 minutes later Grandma told Charles to go check on Ashley, "She's in my room." He walked in and asked, "What are you reading?"

She said, "Your Grandma gave it to me,"

"Charles, do you remember that day you saw me at the cemetery, I asked your mother something? A long time ago she answered my question in this letter."

Charles took the letter and read it.

The Letter

My dear Ashley,

I write this letter one year after we brought Marley home. My mother will keep it in her safe.

Several members of my family know to give this to Marley when she comes of age.

I had a long talk with my son, I know what he did to you was wrong and he has been hurting everyday for that.

He loves you and he is grateful for the beautiful daughter you two have together, even though the way she was conceived was wrong, the love he has for her is so right. Ashley, he loves you even more through her. I'm not sure how old Marley will be when you come looking for her or how old Marley may be when she goes looking for you.

She has a bedtime story about you and she loves to hear it every night before bed, only her daddy can tell it just right.

Many nights I see my son swinging in the gazebo wishing you would walk up. He told me that he is waiting for you to complete his family.

Marley loves you so much. That's all her daddy teaches her. I can't tell you to forgive my son, let your heart tell you what to do. I truly hope I get a chance to meet you, if I do, you will never see this letter. I love you through my son and my granddaughter. She's our heart, and let her be yours. . . .

Stolen Love

Charles said, "I didn't know about this."

Ashley saw a shredder in Grandma's room, she shredded the letter, and they walked back to the dining room together to be with the family.

Tiffany's phone rung, it was the Richards letting her know that the car she sent had picked them up from the airport, and they were in the front yard.

Tiffany said to Grams, "Your surprise guest is here!"

Grams said, "Nobody move, stay right where you are!"

Tiffany looks at Charles and said, "Ashley the surprise is for you."

Ashley thought that her surprise was a stripper. Ashley said to them, "What did you do?"

Grandma came through the door and moved to the side. Ashley saw her mother and father, she stood up and so did Charles.

Charles stood right beside her, Ashley looked at her father, and he opened his arms to her. She went to her father with open arms, hugged him back and her mother, too.

With Charles still standing beside her, Marley got up and stood in front of Tiffany, she knew instantly who they were.

Everyone in the room was happy for Ashley. Tiffany pushed Marley in front of her saying, "This is Marley."

Granddaddy dropped to his knees and held on to his grandbaby.

Grandma touched her on her head; Marley turned and grabbed her grandmother around the waist.

Grams said to the rest of the family, "Let's move to another room."

Charles, Ashley, and her parents stayed in the dining room. Grams said to Marley, "Come with us and let them talk for a while, and you can come back later."

Ashley and her mother, sat at the table holding hands, Charles stood in front of Mr. Richards and he said, "Mr. and Mrs. Richards...I....I..."

Mr. Richards said, "You don't know what to say to us, just like we don't know what to say to our daughter."

Mr. Richards sat down by Ashley and said, "I don't know how to say I'm sorry for taking your little girl away, you wanted her so badly, and I wasn't there for you."

Ashley remembered something Marley said and Ashley had said it to her father. "That was then and now is what matters. Daddy, I just want to start with now."

Mr. Richards said, "Now that's good, now that I have my baby girl back."

Meanwhile Andrew, Linda, and his parents went home, Dru and Charles's Grandpa walked around the ranch.

Tiffany and Grams put the Richards' luggage in the apartment with Marley.

Grams said to Tiffany, "Let's go get them something to eat."

Marley went ahead of them and she peeped through the door asking, "Can I come in?"

Her daddy said, "Sure, Baby!"

She climbed in her granddaddy's lap, talking to him and her grandma while Tiffany and Grams fixed plates of food.

Mr. Richards said to Ashley, "Marley looks like our Marley."

Marley said, "That's my mom's twin sister. I'm keeping her name for her."

Granddaddy says to her, "Yes, you are."

Dru and Grandpa came in and they all sat around the table talking while the Richards ate.

Stolen Love

Later, Grams went to bed saying, "We'll see you all in the morning. Marley, you come with me, young lady, and get ready for bed."

Marley hugged everyone goodnight. Cousin Dru asked, "Do you want me to read you a bedtime story?"

Marley replied, "No!" Looking at her mother, "My bedtime story came true, didn't it Daddy?" Charles answered, "Yes, Baby. It sure did!"

Ashley remembered the letter and said what bedtime story. Charles stood up and kissed Ashley and replied, "You!"

Charles picked up Marley and took her upstairs to her room.

Ashley and Tiffany walked the Richards to the apartment where they would be staying. Then Ashley and Tiffany came back to the house and everyone went to bed.

The next two days the families had fun getting ready for the wedding. On the morning of the 19th, decorators came in to prepare the house for the wedding.

The Reception was to be held on the beautiful terrace. The wedding was to start at 2 pm.

At 10 am, Tiffany left with Marley and Mrs. Richards. Grandma wanted to take her granddaughter shopping because she had missed a lot of birthdays.

When they returned, everybody started getting dressed for the highly anticipated event. After Tiffany and Mrs. Richards got dressed, they went to help Ashley get ready.

Ashley told Tiffany, "Grams hung my wedding dress in a bag behind the door."

Tiffany got the bag and opened it. Ashley exclaimed, "That's not the dress I picked out!"

Ashley's mother said to her, "It's my wedding dress. Tiffany had it altered for you. They added some and took some off."

Ashley said to her mother and Tiffany, "It's beautiful . . . I love it."

The time was suddenly 1:45pm and the wedding was about to start. Ashley walked out to the room where her father was waiting.

She saw all the people that had arrived to be in her wedding. She turned to Tiffany and asked, "What happened to my small wedding?"

Tiffany replied, "You said just the family. We don't have a small family, they're all our cousins."

There were many little boys waiting to escort the little girls, there were about twenty people in the wedding party!

One of her cousins was escorting Marley. Ashley told them they were all so very beautiful. She hugged all of the little children and teenagers.

Ashley said to Tiffany, "I'm sorry for not coming to your wedding, and you did all this for me!" She hugged and thanked Tiffany for everything.

Ashley's father whispered to her, "You are so beautiful. My beautiful baby is getting married." He hugged her, then he hugged Tiffany and said, "Thank you, Tiff, for everything."

The wedding started, Marley came out first with her cousin. Dru stood with Charles, both of them repeating how beautiful Marley was.

The rest of the wedding party entered. As Tiffany entered, Dru told Charles, "I would marry Tiff all over again!"

As the "The Wedding March" played, Charles saw the girl he fell in love with the first time he saw her on that California beach so long ago. He suddenly felt complete.

Everyone gushed about the beautiful dress, dragging so long in the back. Ashley looked around at all the people; she saw Tiffany's parents and several people from the law firm where she worked.

Ashley felt so blessed to have a loving family and friends showing their love for her that it made her cry.

Charles and Ashley wrote their own vows. Charles' vows brought the Richards to tears, the verses were so loving and sweet.

The wedding was so beautiful. Everyone adjourned to the terrace for the reception.

The wedding party was seated.

The bride and groom's first dance was to a song the groom picked for his bride.

The second song the groom selected for his new in-laws. The bridal couple joined the parents of the bride in the dance, then Marley and her escort, and finally all the others joined in.

Charles and Mr. Richards changed partners, and then Charles danced with Marley.

The reception went on until 6 pm.

Charles and Ashley prepared to take a flight that night for their Hawaiian honeymoon. Andrew and Dru took them to the airport.

Mr. Richards decided to fly back in the morning with Tiffany's parents.

Marley was planning to stay with Tiffany and Dru and they would be leaving in four days with Dru's parents.

Suddenly Marley asked, "Daddy . . . Mom . . . can I go with my Grandma and Grandpa until you get back?"

Mr. Richards offered, "We would love to keep her for you." Ashley hesitated.

"Hopefully," Mrs. Richards offered, "Tiffany can pick her up when she gets back. . . ."

Ashley slowly shook her head no. Her Mother implored, "Please, Baby, give me these four days."

Suddenly something came over Ashley making her say, "That was then." Charles chimed in and said, "Sure you can!"

Stolen Love

Mr. Richards said to Charles, "When you come back, and when you're ready for her to come home, I would love to take her back to Promise and spend some more time with her there."

Charles answered, "That will complete my family."

He picked up Marley and said, "We'll see the three of you in two weeks."

Ashley walked away and looked to the sky and said "Thank you, Mrs. Roxenbury,"

Then she heard, "And, thank you, Mrs. Roxenbury."

Ashley smiled as she walked up to Charles and hugged him. He held her close to him as if it were twenty degrees outside.

Mr. Richards looked at them and said, "That completes my family."

She hugged her parents goodbye and bent down to Marley, saying, "I love you! We are going to have so much fun with Grandma and Grandpa when we get home."

She hugged, kissed, and told her mother she would see her in two weeks and have fun.

Andrew and Dru took the new Mr. and Mrs. Roxenbury to the airport while Tiffany visited with her parents.

The family invited the Richards back to their home the next year since they were now all one family.

The Richards went back to pack.

Marley followed them telling them about her ranch, her horse, the new saddle that her Gramps made for her birthday, how she and her parents rode around the ranch, and all about the go-carts.

Chapter Six

The next morning, the Richard's and the McKinley's flew back home with Marley.

When the Richards arrived home, Grandma told Marley, "You can put your things in your mother's room."

Grandma showed her the door to the room. Marley entered the room as grandpa was coming down the hall.

Marley slowly looked around the room and saw that grandma had framed and hung all of her mother drawings on the walls.

Marley started putting her things away and saw her mother's photo album. In the album, she found pictures of her grandparents, the twins when they were babies, and Ashley and Tiffany when they were her age.

She told Grandpa, "I look like my mother then, but she looks different now."

She kept turning through the book-asking grandpa to name everyone.

On the last pages of the book, she saw pictures of her parents at the amusement park and on the beach with Tiffany and Dru.

Grandma came in and Marley told them the bedtime story her daddy told her; just by looking at the pictures, even the funny things her mother did at the beach and about Ashley cheating at the amusement park games.

Marley saw in pictures, what her daddy had always told her. Grandma told Marley she could take the book home with her, it was her gift.

Monday morning Grandpa left for work, kissing Marley, and saying, "I'll see you this evening."

Grandma owned her own shop where she sold her drawings and knick-knacks. Marley went to work with her each day.

Marley spied some drawings on the wall in her grandma's office that grandma drew. Beside them was a drawing that Ashley drew.

Marley told grandma that she drew and painted, too.

Marley asked grandma, "Can I draw a picture for you?"

Grandma said, "Sure you can, when you finish it I'll hang it next to your mother's."

She took Marley back in her workshop and gave her everything she needed.

Each day they came to the shop Marley went in the back room to work on the picture. At the end of the week, Marley finished her painting.

Marley tells Grandma, "It's finished, but it's still wet!"

Grandma went in the back to look at Marley's artwork.

She saw a beautiful painting of Ashley and Marley together. Marley painted it from a picture her daddy took of them by the lake.

Grandma hugged her grandchild telling her it was beautiful.

She told Marley, "Your mother started drawing when she was your age. We will let it dry over the weekend and hang it Monday morning."

Grandma had painted a picture of her twins. Ashley had chosen to paint a picture of her parents. Now, Marley had painted a picture herself and Ashley. All of the paintings were hanging on the wall in Grandma's shop.

Grandma and Marley went home after a long week of working at the shop. Marley saw the kids next door playing, she asked, "Can I go play with them?"

Grandma said, "Yes, I'm going to make dinner."

Saturday morning, Grandpa told Marley that they were taking her to see the town where her mother grew up.

"It's where Tiffany lives. You can go see her, too." Grandma added.

They drove around town showing Marley where they used to live.

The Richards spent the day with Tiffany's parents, while Tiffany and Cousin Dru took Marley to the Amusement Park.

She had a lot of fun with Tiffany and Dru. They told her about all the times they went there with her mom and dad. Marley went home with lots of stuffed animals she won or Tiffany and Dru won for her.

It was Marley's last week with her grandparents.

She spent evenings looking through her mother's things, gathering what she wanted to take them back home with her to California.

Thursday morning Marley received a phone call from her parents. They called to let her know that they are home from their honeymoon and they would see her in two days.

Marley and Grandma cleaned the house and got ready to go to the shop. When they arrived, they opened the shop and started redecorating it. They also painted pictures for Marley to take home with her.

Grandma told Marley, "It's getting late. Let's go start supper."

When they got home, Granddaddy had already cooked supper! He surprised them with food, music, and flowers.

They ate, sang, and danced to the songs on the radio.

Friday morning grandma took Marley shopping, and then they went to Granddaddy's office since she wanted to see where he worked.

Granddaddy took them out for lunch, while eating, Granddaddy asked Marley, "Are you ready to go home tomorrow?"

She answered, "Yes, I want to see my mom, dad, and my horse."

The Richards and Marley finished their lunch and Granddaddy went back to work.

Grandma and Marley went to the shop for a couple of hours more and then went home. Saturday morning Mr. Richards called Ashley to let her know that they were leaving.

A few hours later Marley was back home. Happy to see her parents, she ran to them and they all unloaded the car.

When Marley finished unpacking her things she went to check on her horse while her parents made lunch.

The Roxenburys and the Richards had lunch in the yard by the lake. Later that evening they all went horseback riding.

The Richards stayed until Sunday afternoon. Charles invited them to come back anytime they wanted to visit.

Granddaddy told Marley, "We'll see you in three weeks for the weekend. You call us anytime!"

They all said their goodbyes.

Marley spent the rest of the day telling her parents about the photo album pictures, working at the shop, visiting Tiffany and Cousin Dru, drawing pictures and hanging them in grandma's shop, and how she met some friends next door to the Richards.

One year later, Ashley made partner at the Law Firm on the same day that Tiffany gave birth to her first child.

Tiffany and Dru named their first-born Andrew Tyrek Roxenbury, IV.

The Richards visit Promise five times a year for the weekends and they join the rest of the family in Texas once a year for summer vacation.

Author

Joyce Lomax-Dukes, of the baby-boomer generation, was born and reared in Altamonte Springs, Florida. She was the 17th of 18 children of David and Annie Mae Lomax. Her late sister Jean was both a songwriter and poet. Her oldest brother,  Nathaniel, is the author of another Olmstead Publishing book, "Jesus is Calling You."

Joyce mothered four adult children, fifteen grandchildren, and four great grandchildren. She enjoys spending time with her family and friends and writing poems and short stories. She is a hard worker and loves communicating with new people. Joyce was a supervisor of new construction clean up and involved in retirement home cleaning.

www.ingramcontent.com/pod-product-compliance
Lightning Source LLC
Chambersburg PA
CBHW071406170626
46811CB00003B/1275